The Midnight Kid

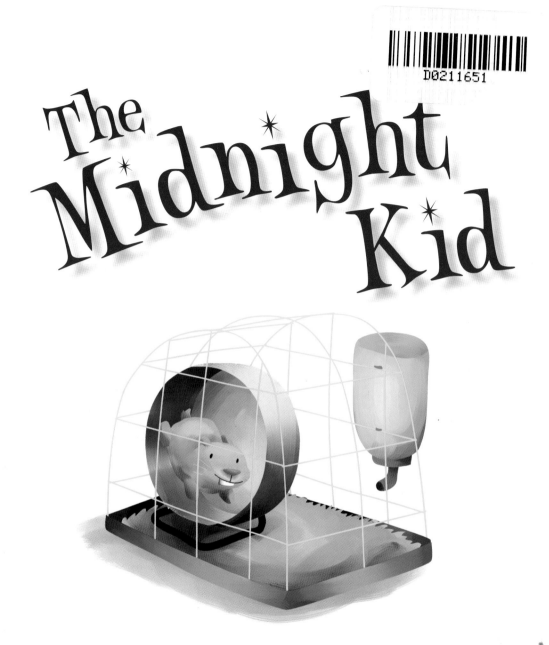

by Nan Walker
illustrated by Barry Gott

Kane Press, Inc.
New York

To Mia and Ava—N.W.
For Nandi—B.G.

Acknowledgements: Our thanks to Jessica Steinitz, Research Manager, National Sleep Foundation, for helping to make this book as accurate as possible.

Library of Congress Cataloging-in-Publication Data

Walker, Nan.
  The Midnight Kid / by Nan Walker ; illustrated by Barry Gott.
    p. cm. — (Science solves it!)
  Summary: When Peter sees a movie about super-smart aliens who never sleep, he decides to stay awake for a few nights so he will become super-smart too.
    ISBN-13: 978-1-57565-238-2 (alk. paper)
    ISBN-10: 1-57565-238-2 (alk. paper)
    [1. Sleep—Fiction.]   I. Gott, Barry, ill. II. Title.
  PZ7.W153643Mi 2007
  [E]—dc22
                                                    2006026409

10 9 8 7 6 5 4 3 2 1

First published in the United States of America in 2007 by Kane Press, Inc.
Printed in Hong Kong.

Science Solves It! is a registered trademark of Kane Press, Inc.

Book Design: Edward Miller

www.kanepress.com

"*Puny earthling, you have spent 37,525 hours of your life asleep—like a mindless slug. No wonder your brain is so tiny—*"

"Peter!" my dad says. "Time for bed!"

Oh, no. Just when the movie was getting good. "Can't I stay up to watch the end?" I beg. "It's summer vacation."

Dad shakes his head. "You need your rest."

Grumbling, I go off to brush my teeth.

"The aliens on Planet Zoltan never sleep at all," I tell my mom. "That's why they're so advanced. They spend all that extra time getting smarter and smarter."

I'm hoping Mom will take the hint and let me stay up late, but all she says is, "You have toothpaste on your chin."

"Don't the aliens get sleepy?" asks my little brother, Lenny.

"Nope," I tell him. "They don't need sleep."

"Why not?"

I shrug. "Maybe they trained themselves bit by bit. You know, a little less sleep each night."

Lenny looks worried. "How do they know when it's time for breakfast?"

"It's only a movie, kiddo," Dad says.

> **Did You Know?**
> Just how much do humans sleep? About three thousand hours a year. And kids sleep even more than that!

Mom and Dad kiss us both good night, turn out the light, and shut the door.

I lie awake in the dark, thinking about the super-smart aliens on Planet Zoltan.

Maybe it *is* just a movie, but it sure makes sense to me. Imagine all the things I could be doing if I didn't have to sleep!

I could work on the deluxe monster-truck model kit I got for my birthday.

I could teach my hamster, Twinkie, some cool tricks.

Maybe I could even learn to find a few constellations, like the Great Bear.

No doubt about it. Sleep is a waste of time.

The next day, I start my No Sleep Campaign. "Don't you want me to be super smart?" I ask my dad.

"No," he says. "I like you the way you are."

I think he's teasing me.

"Just imagine the things I could get done," I tell Mom.

"Like cleaning your room?" she asks.

That's not exactly what I had in mind.

By dinnertime, I'm getting desperate.

"I could learn Swahili," I say. "I could study rocket science."

Dad looks at Mom. "It *is* summer vacation," he says. "Maybe we should let him stay up a few nights. He might learn something."

I wonder if he means science or Swahili?

Did You Know?
Your brain is actually working hard while you're fast asleep. Scientists think that while you're snoozing, your brain is sorting and storing all kinds of information.

9

They tell me the rules: No watching TV all night. No loud noises. And stay out of the bedroom so Lenny can sleep.

Mom adds, "Three nights is the limit, Peter—if you last that long."

"Can I stay up, too?" Lenny begs.

"Sorry, pal," says Dad. "One space-alien genius in the family is quite enough."

Don't Try This at Home
(or anywhere else!)
The world record for staying awake was set by 17-year-old Randy Gardner. He didn't sleep for 11 days! But it was no picnic. After a few days, Randy was so tired he couldn't even focus his eyes to watch TV. Ouch!

I move Twinkie's cage downstairs so we can hang out without waking up Lenny.

"Want to watch a movie?" Mom asks me. "It's called *Love Under the Weeping Willow*."

Yuck! "No, thanks," I say. "I'm going to read the dictionary." I only have three nights, so I'd better start getting super smart right away.

"Tonight I'm staying up with you!" I tell Twinkie. Hamsters are nocturnal. That means Twinkie sleeps all day, then runs on her wheel at night.

"Look, Twinkie," I tell her. "An aardvark is nocturnal, just like you."

She blinks at me. I think she understands.

Aa

Aardvark

Night Owls and Early Birds
What do owls, bats, cats, mice, toads, and insects like fireflies and crickets all have in common? They're **nocturnal**. They sleep during the day and stay awake at night. (And no matter how late you like to stay up, humans are the opposite. We're **diurnal**!)

"Abelmosk is a bushy herb that grows—"
YAWN. "Grows in Asia and—" HUGE YAWN.
"And the East Indies. Isn't that interesting?"

Twinkie shows me her furry rear end.
Hmm, maybe it's time to put down the
dictionary. Memorizing will be easier
tomorrow, anyway. I'll be smarter by then.

I open Twinkie's cage. "Let's go out and look
at the stars," I say.

Outside, the night air feels heavy on my arms and legs, and the sky is a deep navy blue. I stare up at the stars, trying to connect the dots. Is that the Big Dipper or the Little Dipper?

Suddenly Twinkie squirms out of my hands. She jumps to the ground and takes off. I can't see her anywhere!

"Twinkie!" I yell. "Here, girl! Twinkie!"

The deck lights snap on, and my dad calls, "What's going on out here?"

Just then I spot Twinkie and scoop her up. "Nothing," I say. "We're looking at the stars."

"Better come in, Peter," Dad says. "It's late."

I put Twinkie back in her cage and flop
down on the couch. She gave me a real scare!

Now that my heart has quit beating so fast,
I feel kind of tired. Maybe I'll just rest for a
minute. . . .

When I open my eyes, Lenny is standing over me. "You fell asleep!" he says.

I try to look as if I did it on purpose. "I'm training myself bit by bit, remember? Tonight I'll stay up all night."

After breakfast, I go to play baseball with my friend D.J. When I strike out for the third time, D.J. asks, "What's up with you?"

I tell her about my No Sleep Campaign.

"It sure isn't helping your swing," she says.

"True," I reply. "But I'll bet you don't know what an abelmosk is."

"No. What is it?"

"It's a . . . it's a . . . Hmm. I can't remember."

Strike Three, You're Out!

You reach for a glass and—*crash!*—you spill milk everywhere. Are you just clumsy, or do you need more sleep? Too little sleep can make you a big klutz—especially when you're doing physical activities like playing sports.

That afternoon, I help my dad put up the birdhouse he's been building.

"Feeling smarter yet?" he asks after I hand him the wrong tool for the third time.

To tell the truth, I'm not feeling super smart at all. I'd better try extra hard to stay awake tonight. I only have two nights left!

No Snoring in Class
When teachers tell you to get lots of sleep the night before a test, do it! If you're overtired, you're more likely to make mistakes and have trouble following directions. (Besides, your classmates won't like it if you snore.)

It's quiet in the house. I set up a clock so I can keep track of time.

Ten o'clock. An hour past my bedtime, and I'm still going strong. This is a cinch!

Ten-thirty. I start to feel sleepy, so I fix myself a little snack.

Eleven-fifteen. Maybe a few jumping jacks will perk me up.

Almost midnight. Twinkie is still running on her wheel. Where does she get all that energy?

Maybe I'll just take a little nap. But this time I set the alarm clock so I won't sleep too long. See? I'm already smarter.

Tired—or Wired?
Exercising, drinking caffeine, watching TV or playing computer games . . . If you do any of these things too close to bedtime, you could be tossing and turning all night!

"Peter, what in the world are you doing?"

My whole family is standing in the kitchen. Is it morning? "The alarm clock must be broken," I say. "It never went off."

"It certainly did," Mom says, crossing her arms. "And woke everyone up."

Lenny giggles. "Everyone but you."

Mom tells me to go straight to bed—and no more all-nighters. I'm too sleepy to argue.

In the morning, though, I have more energy.
"It's not fair!" I say. "You promised I could have three nights!"

"You promised no loud noises," Mom says, looking tired and cranky. "You may think sleep is a waste of time, but I don't."

In the end, she agrees to let me stay awake one more night—but without my alarm clock.

Crankypants!

Did you wake up feeling groggy this morning? Did you beg for five more minutes in bed? Did you throw a tantrum because someone ate all the Frostee Crisp cereal? You probably stayed up too late last night. Not getting enough sleep makes people grumpy!

Space Cadet!
Have you ever finished a page in your book and then realized you have no idea what you just read? Do your teacher's words ever sound like gibberish because you can't concentrate? Lack of sleep can make it hard for you to focus or make decisions.

That evening, I play checkers with my dad. Usually I can beat him easily. Tonight, though, I seem to be having trouble paying attention.

"King me!" Dad says.

After everyone goes to bed, I get to work on my monster truck. I've got almost all the parts in place. Now I just have to glue—

AAARGH! I can't believe this. I broke the windshield.

When did I get so clumsy?

Maybe a little TV will take my mind off the truck disaster. I promised not to watch TV all night, but just one show won't count.

I flip through the channels.

Hey! It's *Crash-Land on Planet Zoltan*. Now I can finally see how it ends.

The alien is just about to zap Hugo the Boy Astronaut, when . . .

I can't believe it. The Zoltanians were *robots*!
No wonder they never needed to sleep!

Maybe if they could sleep, their super-smart robot brains wouldn't wear out so fast.
I'll have to think it over. . . .

I wonder if I could use these parts to fix my spaceship.

After I've had a good night's sleep.

Recharge!

Babies need 10–18 hours of sleep a night. Five- to twelve-year-olds need 10–11 hours (this means YOU!). Adults need 7–9 hours. Some people need more sleep than others, but everyone needs to recharge—even robots!

THINK LIKE A SCIENTIST

Peter thinks like a scientist—and so can you!

Observing is something you do all the time—except when you're sleeping, of course! When you observe, you use your senses to check things out. Everyone observes. In fact, it's hard *not* to. Just try it!

Look Back

- On page 17, what does Peter observe about how he feels? Why do you think he feels this way?
- What does Peter observe on pages 20–21. Why do you think his behavior changes?
- What does he observe about his energy level on page 24? What about on page 25? What do you think happened?

Try This!

Observe your own behavior!

Make a Sleep Chart. For one week, write down what time you go to bed and what time you wake up. Figure out how many hours of sleep you got each night. Then write down how you're feeling the next day—in the morning, in the afternoon, and in the evening.

Bonus! Have a friend or family member observe you, too—but don't tell them how much sleep you're getting. Do you think they can guess?

8 hours	10 hours	11 hours

Blahhh	A-OK	Wonder Woman!